Tales of ONE-STAR-LIGHT

E-L-Paula

@one-star-light

Copyright © 2014 Erika Linhares de Paula

Published by OM42-Gateway Limited
www.one-star-light.com

All rights reserved. No part of this book may be reproduced, stored, or transmitted by any means—whether auditory, graphic, mechanical, or electronic—without written permission of both publisher and author, except in the case of brief excerpts used in critical articles and reviews. Unauthorized reproduction of any part of this work is illegal and is punishable by law.

ISBN: 978-0-9928259-0-4 (sc)
ISBN: 978-0-9928259-1-1 (e)

Library of Congress Control Number: 2014902306

Because of the dynamic nature of the Internet, any web addresses or links contained in this book may have changed since publication and may no longer be valid. The views expressed in this work are solely those of the author and do not necessarily reflect the views of the publisher, and the publisher hereby disclaims any responsibility for them.

Any people depicted in stock imagery provided by Thinkstock are models, and such images are being used for illustrative purposes only. Certain stock imagery © Thinkstock.

To my "frach-ether-nals"

As the Tales of One-Star-Light " be-comes" "One" in matter, I manifest into words my gratitude to "Each-One" and " All-One" of you, who contributed for the story to takes its "One-action-form" in "Earth-lands".

"Gratias vobis ago"

E-L-Paula-Y-R & T-B-A-N - "Earth-lands" - Fall - MMXIII -AD

ONE
ARE YOU
:
YOU ARE
ONE

CHAPTER ONE OF TWELVE

Star-lights in Heaven

"One are you- You are One"

Hi,

I am Yhkhree-Ra.

Nice to meet you.... Again!

I am sure we have met before at some point in one of the countless existing time-spaces in this immense place we live that we know as the "Uni-verse"!

I come from a far distant galaxy, way beyond even the most advanced astronomic civilisations can trace or access.

In "Earth-lands' " conceptualisation, my kind can be described as stars.

All I can tell you is that in our living reality, people of my kind experience ourselves as "One-Star-Light"!

From the essence of who I am, I share my Light in the here and now with you.

As you share some of my experiences in this book, you will be connected to the essence of "The-One".

It might be the case that you are "One", like us , already , but for your own reasons you have chosen to forget that identity of "your- One- self" for a while!

In any case, whoever you truly are...

Welcome to this little journey!

It is tricky to explain the Origin of "The-One-origin".

I will try my best.

Do not worry too much in comprehend the science behind it! Try reading this as novel or if you are a romantic, like me, a love story!

Perhaps, it feels lighter this way!

And for sure much brighter!

Enjoy your wonders...

May the light be with you!

"One are you- You are One"

ONE
IN ALL
:
ALL IN
ONE

CHAPTER TWO OF TWELVE

The Seeds of Countless Time

"One in All - All in One"

"The-One" is where my kind originated from. In that sense, you may perceive us as the "little Ones" or "the children of The-One".

Nominations apart, we are known as the One of "The -One".

At one point in time, past, present and future became "The- One"; the existence of the non-existence!

Many of you may think: that's non-sense!

You may be surprised but you are absolutely right! It is all about non-sense!

This is the exactly nature of what, or who "The-One" is: non-sense in the sense that "all is nothing" and at the same time "all is everything"!

Following the "Uni-verse's" laws of expansion and integration, our kind's galactic structure was integrated to several different planets as to spread the seeds of "Uni-versal" love and progressive evolution.

In that sense, all of our kind, which descends from "The-One" are "One" amongst and within "our-One-self".

We were all "uni-ted" by a "sacred -light -con-science", known as "Khris-Thy", who guides and protects all of us through space and time.

Religion for us in the far away realms, translates in its Latin "Earth-lands' " word "re-ligare", which seems to imply "re-linking" the Creature to the Creator.

Using our terms of reference, it means making the link between "One "and "The- One".

As descendants of a high hierarchy of Angels of Light, our evolution was centred on integrating to different physical states of being in the thirty-three dimensions of the material world.

Some of these civilisations in which our "One" seeds were spread were more advanced than others but none of them were or indeed are so far, classified as "non-physical quantum". Therefore, they cannot reach "The-One" neither ascend to it.

So far, none of the known planets and galaxies, as a "Uni-Thy" of "The-One", has reached the ethereal " status-quo" of pure light of love. None has ascended as a collective as yet!

They are all trying hard thought, at their own collective's pace.

This is the beauty of evolution!

There is a time and a space for all creatures, living and non-living to reach "The -One".

One day.... Some Time...

So far, as a consequence , "The-One's " evolution is limited to the return of us, "the seeded - Ones" as individuals , in the hope that at some point, in "time-space", a great number of planets and galaxies will be integrated to "The-One" as a complete "Uni-ty".

More "The-One" grows bigger: More understanding ...More compassion ...More light

As for the time being, only the "One" with the seeds of "The-One" can ascend back to the light source.

The vision of descending was to create, out of "The-One", more seeds of "One", so more would become part of "The-One". Hence, "The-One" would keep expanding its "Uni-versal" love and light throughout the "in-finity "of the "Uni-verse".

More "The-One" grows bigger: More light .... More pure energy ... More love

From this far distant place, countless time-spaces ago, a great number of "the seeded-Ones" from "The-One" was then spread into different locations across the "Uni-verse".

Only a few of these locations can be identified in the actual time in which I tell you this story as many locations are still unknown to "Earth-lands" , many of them already ceased to exist, many of them are still to be born!

In this sense, past, present and future all become "One"; "One" becomes nothing!

Here, I make a remark for the readers of other planets and galaxies nearby:

Please do not forget that you all have a great deal of learning yet to develop!

Do not be misguided by the idea that you are more evolved than others or others are more evolved than you!

Evolution is endless and for "All" independent of the stage of evolution in which "One" is.

So, focus on the mission you have chosen. The pathway must be made of love and compassion.

This is the only way to Light!

"The-One" is waiting for you to be "re-united"!

All is moving and evolving, regardless the points of reference.

"One in All: All in One"

ONE
IS ONE:
ONE IS
ONE

CHAPTER THREE OF TWELVE

Soul mates

"One is one - One is One"

This is where and when my love story starts in this story telling!

I am not tracing it back from the beginning of my beginning. Also, it probably will not have an ending that you imagine!

To date, I cannot figure out the ending myself!

The only thing I can say is that in the "here and now" my "One-beloved- Star-Light-prince" is not yet physically by my side!

Let's hope he joins me soon, hopefully in one of the next chapters!

I miss him! BIG TIME!

I keep wondering where my "One-Star-Light-prince" is. My "human heart" is endlessly searching for him. In the other hand, my "One-Star-Light-soul" knows deep down that we are synchronised, and it is just a matter of connecting once we are both ready to return to complete our promised mission in "Earth-lands".

Later, I will tell you more of what happened!

This journey is all about what I can recall in the here and now!

As "Time" does not exist, some bits of my memories come from the past, others from the present and others from the future!

What a mix!

So, let's start!

From "The-One-source", Yhkhree-Ra, who happens to be me, descended. I was given light amongst many others, all connected parts of "The-One".

We were created to be the "female-One" and the "male-One". We are then the counter-parts of "One": "One-half" and "One-half".

Soul - mates, this is the closest word that can describe the significance of two becoming "One".

The connection between two beings that forms "One " is of an "ether-nal" nature, indissoluble, connected through pure love. This form of love can only be experienced when "One & One" are back to "The- One".

However, the manifestation of other forms of love and relationships is in line with the "Uni-verse" laws of attraction and free will.

From the origin of origins, I descended as a princess from "The-One". I was seeded in the Orion Constellation, as linked to the vibrational energies of "All-nit-Ahkh", which is one of the three stars that can be seen in the Orion Belt. I was named by the Orions as Thyan-B-Ahkh-Naton.

My soul mate, Ahrgyan-Sy-Ahkh-Naton was also seeded in the Orion constellation but in a different area, currently described as M42 Nebula.

Both of us, amongst many others "Ones", were protected and guided by the galactic and cosmic guardians responsible for the expansion of "The-One" in the Orion Constellation.

The cosmic masters of Orion, under the Elder Galactic Council, became the 'temporary' guardians of the "Ones" seeded in their constellation.

The learning of the "Ones" was co-ordinated by the Sidereal Masters who overlook Orion and other nearby constellations.

In the material realms, we all have to follow the evolution grading according to the thirty-three sacred levels and dimensions of the "Uni-versal" progression.

After this cycle completes itself, it is then time for each one of us, as a " Uni-Thy" of the "Uni-Thy" to finally return home.

We both, Thyan and Ahrgyan were bright learners from the stars. We were settled and together with other "Ones", we grew individually and collectively. So did Orion as an evolving system.

More light back to "The-One" source, more living energy is created...

We were at the same time, brilliant "One-Star-Light- students" and wise "cosmic-masters".

And of course we were so in love as we were meant to be...inseparable in hearts, thoughts and soul.

All you can imagine about a perfect match, it was there and much more...

Yes, it is true! True love stories do exist! The happy ending though, sometimes is kept on hold...

So far, so good! Love is still in the air...

Even in the "here and now", I can feel in my heart and soul all my love for my beautiful "One-Star-Light-prince". I am sure he can feel the same as well.

Even apart, we were, are and always will be together for ever and ever, again and again.

May the Angels of Light say: "A-men".

"One is one - One is One"

ONE
IS HALF
:
HALF IS
ONE

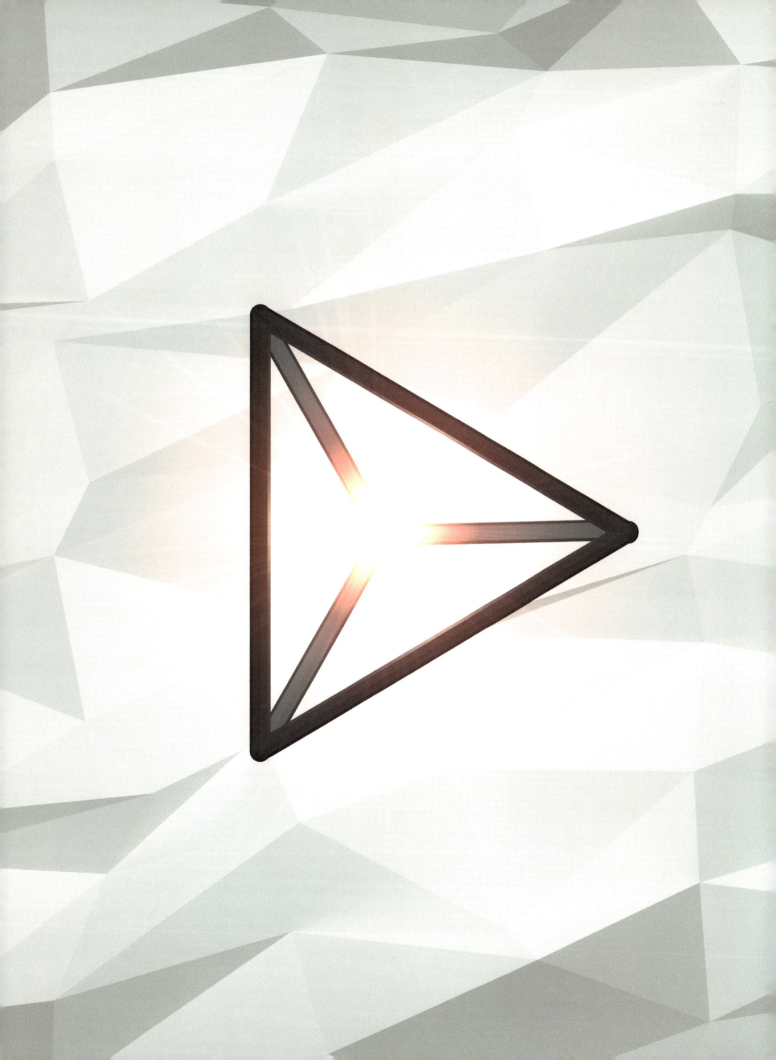

CHAPTER FOUR OF TWELVE

Love is forever

"One is Half - Half is One"

Most of the time, we seem to take gifts from the "Uni-verse" as granted!

Even us, "One-Star-Lights"!

As we were born meant to be "One" in "One", Ahrgyan and I, never paid much attention to the gift of our "never-ending" or "ever-lasting"" friend-partner-love-ship".

We were just so happy and contained in our "relation-ship" that enjoying every moment of it was a joy! And I can tell you from my heart, we truly "en-joyed" it!

Love in the "One-Star-Light- dimension" is pure in essence!

Like two "candles-lights" that mingle, going through each other and yet keeping their "One-individuality".

Like two "candle-lights" that dance in perfect harmony, following the flow of the "Uni-verse" in its glory!

Like two "candle-lights" that feel "every -thing" and become "One-thing" in a moment of "ether-nity"!

All was perfect and perfect was absolutely fine for us!

"One-Star-Light-princess" loves her "One-Star-Light-prince" who loves his "One-Star-Light-princess".

All is as it should be!

Who, in all senses, would change perfection anyway?

Love is "Uni-versal"; so is its language!

My "One-Star-Light-prince" and I are so much "One"; so much in love...

So is it for each "One" of you!

You also have your soul-mate who lives forever in the kingdom of your heart!

If you were not lucky enough to have your soul- mate with you in the here and now, you are at the exact stage as I am: searching...

Countless fairy-tales...

Regardless of anything, love is our dream and at the same time it is our way.

One look, one movement, one word....

That's all we need to have our souls connected...

No word can describe this feeling of "be-longing"; of complementing "each and One-other".

I hope my "One-Star-Light-prince", wherever he is now, can recall this feeling.

Moreover, I hope that he can feel my presence as I can feel his.

My human heart is so lonely now...

I pray for the "Uni-verse" to bring him back to my world...

Or that he comes to my rescue...

So the order of things can be re-established "for-ever" again ...

What about you? Can your soul remember the "other-One-half"?

Perhaps this is the meaning of what you are looking for...

Perhaps that's why you have so many lovers and yet, have not yet found your "One-love".

Believe, your soul-mate is there, somewhere...

Like me, just waiting to be "re-united"!

Believe: Love is "for-ever"...

"One is Half - Half is One"

ONE
IS OTHER
:
OTHER IS
ONE

CHAPTER FIVE OF TWELVE

The bright side of the darkness

"One is Other - Other is One"

Light could never exist without the darkness.

Darkness could never exist without light.

They not only complement each other but also are part of "The-One" as "One Uni-Thy" of the "Uni-verse" evolution.

So, exactly like "some-Ones" are known as "One-Star-Light", "other -Ones" are known as "The Darks".

This tale is not about a battle of one side against the other!

It is all about balance!

Remember this is a love story, not a galactic battle fiction!

So, in this story there are no "goodies or baddies", but "beings of Light" who were originated from the same source, that fall apart and one day, once this is all sorted, will be "re-united".

The same way as the "One-Star-Lights"," The Darks" descended to many galaxies, constellations and planets. The only difference was that they forgot that they were originated from the same source, from the "The-One".

"The Darks" were and still are under the illusion they can overcome their own Creator.

Hence, "The Darks" are not necessary bad neither the "One-Star-Lights" are necessary good. They all simply are what or who they are: an integrant part of the "The-One".

Through my life journeys in "Earth-lands", one of the lessons I have to learn quickly was about the limitations of humans' dialectic and tri-dimensional world in which they live.

Concepts such as good and bad, right and wrong, black and white and so on are restrictive and misleading.

The terms, which I am portraying in these memories, as for example" The Darks" and "One-Star-Light", man and woman, prince and princess, only follow this dual model so as to facilitate the representation of complex concepts and models that are yet to be experienced by human kind.

"The Darks" , seeking perfection in "be-coming" Creators themselves, developed the human race with combined genes, which they thought would be perfect to create a massive slavery of souls to satisfy their desire to "be-come" "The-One".

What they still have to understand is that they are already part of "The-One".

To date, they sustain this false illusion. However, like any "Earth-lands' "laws or principles, this belief is temporary.

Therefore, like for all the rest of us in the "Uni-verse", there is only one way which will lead all of us to be "re-united" to "The-One". No matter how many diversions we choose to take, on which side we choose to be, we all going to be "re-united" there, regardless...

One Day- One Time.

As a way of controlling mankind, "The Darks" created genetic triggers, powerful enough to maintain control and to suppress unwanted behaviour. They aimed to restrict the natural flow of the "Uni-verse - laws" to include free-will and freedom.

They portrayed themselves as Gods that punish; they created restrictive social frameworks to contain the freedom of being; they established self-regulators concepts such as guilt and sins, that overshadow the "Uni-versal" principles of love and compassion.

The day that "The Darks" were able to develop mankind, with "con-science", feelings and free will, "The Darks" felt they no longer needed "The-One". What "The Darks" did not consider was that once free, mankind will no longer need "The Darks".

"The Darks", when creating mankind, were too arrogant to dismiss one of the "Uni-versal" laws: "All is One ", regardless of their origin. Mistakenly, they denied the "Supreme -The-One". They naively thought that by developing a new race, they could be God themselves.

The flaw in "The Darks' "plans was that, mankind inevitably contain the fractals genes of "The-One", which could not be isolated by their science. This was and still is beyond of "The Darks' "control. This is the sacred legacy from the "The- One", which gives mankind its ticket to freedom if they so wish.

The bottom line is that their beings, like all of us in the "Universe", Dark, Light, Grey, Green ... will have to evolve and return back to our "Origin"; to return to the "The-One".

That is the only way for "All" of us!

"One is Other - Other is One"

ONE
IS "UNI-THY"
∶
"UNI-THY" IS ONE

CHAPTER SIX OF TWELVE

Missionaries in "Earth-lands"

"One is "Uni-thy" - "Uni-thy" is One"

"One" would think "One" was prepared for the mission in the "Blue-Planet".

Yes, the Orions have prepared us!

The Orions trusted us to do embrace such divine mission!

We were confident that we would succeed.

We downgraded our light and vibrational energy levels again to be able to live in "Earth-lands".

However, our grading was still very high for the planet's standards.

For that reason, we should be careful and respectful of both, the "Uni-verse" and "Earth-lands' laws"!

Difficult task indeed, when you are totally exposed to the multitude and diversity of "Earth-lands- life"!

This is a challenge in itself, as the "Uni-versal" laws are unique and absolute in contrast to the Earth-lands' laws", which are too many ... And too volatile .... And so temporal!

This could potentially be a huge trap for a curious and adventurous "One-Star-Light- princess" like me!

The mission was and still is to experience human life, to help mankind to evolve to freedom of their souls, to spread the teachings of love and compassion. If there is one "Earth-lands- word" that could express our mission, this word would be "enlightenment".

How this could be done? For how long? What would be the strategy of the mission? What would be the mission of the mission?

You may be thinking: such advanced kind like you, you probably should be able to predict the outcome of what you would like to achieve.

All I can say is that this is a big assumption of yours!

Neither we, nor the Orions had the capability of predicting the outcome of a mission, which had so many unpredictable and unstable variables.

One thing we learned quite quickly about mankind was not to underestimate the power of their genus!

Human beings are enduring, quick learners and extremely adaptable to the unknown. They have an unique capability of developing resilience, strength and compassion.

These and other qualities make them capable of turning against their own "gene-rator";

These and other qualities are the ones that will lead them to Light.

This dormant power inside each one of the humans is so intrinsically diverse and inter-wined that it cannot be translated in to pure science, laws and equations.

This is the core of our "One-Star-Light" learning: to better understand the diversity of the unknown.

You may think what is then the core of our mission?

It is to assist mankind to free themselves so they could follow their way to the stars too!

The challenge, is to adapt advanced technology and knowledge in ways that mankind could experience and learn in its on time and at their own pace.

As you can now picture , at the same time that this mission is descending for us as a means of reaching our targeted evolution ; for mankind and other kinds , our downgrading was a way forward to their evolution , in other words: ascending!

What a "Uni-verse" of contradiction we live! Ascending, descending....

I particularly love being part of it!

After all, after so long being amongst the Orions and other kinds to include mankind, I am sure my "One-Star-Light-genetic-print" have changed; better saying they definitely evolved!

As a bubbly "One-Star-Light", I can say that I am very proud of having a little bit of all of that!

Back to the mission in "Earth-lands" ...

Missions like this were confined to few of us with the knowledge and wisdom to overcome the implications of "One-self" settling on lower vibrational energetic fields.

This is a risky and dangerous choice as once caught in the wheel of "human-living", as we nicknamed "hamster-wheel " we would be basically surviving in a hostile and unknown environment with restricted support from our "Sidereal Mentors".

"Our - One" (myself and Ahrgyan) and many "others-Ones", who were also part of our group descended. Progressively, we started stepping down to "Earth-lands" in different stages, dimensions and places, depending on what we agreed to do.

In this unknown world, the only thing of which we were absolutely sure was that we will have to complete the mission, regardless of the frames of time and space in which it was confined.

After all, we will return to Orion to report back on the material realms so then, at any point we so wish, to ascend back to "The-One".

Time to go to "Earth-lands" now!

Before leaving, one last view of "Earth-lands" from far distance!

What a beautiful "Blue-Planet"!

That image and my feelings of love, gratitude and respect for this incredibly stunning Planet is printed in my soul.

"For-ever"....

It is too overwhelming to describe.

"Earth-lands" from distance is absolutely spectacular, so peaceful, a tyne gem of this solar system!

We hold hands and off we go...

"One is "Uni-thy" - "Uni-thy" is One"

ONE
IS LIGHT
:
DARK IS
ONE

CHAPTER SEVEN OF TWELVE

Broken vows

"One is Light - Dark is One"

The mission in "Earth-lands" started.

All the assignments planned had a peaceful and strategic objective. They meant no harm to "any-One", living or non-living being, in "Heaven" or "Earth-lands".

All of us, whom agreed to take part in the mission in "Earth-lands" made a solemn vow of loyalty and commitment to the "Uni-versal" Laws.

Our group was based at a huge "satellite-basis" called "Attalah-Thys".

Its location was under sea but in a different dimension so we could not be tracked by either "The Darks" or their collaborators.

We could move to any place in "Earth-lands" either in its physical dimension or through any other higher vibrational energy fields connected to the planet.

It was a fascinating experience for us, moving from low to high vibrational states, which made our work extremely complex but very rewarding.

We had access to Portals of "Space-Time-Energy" that could transport us between places, dimensions, stars, whatever, whenever, however we so wished!

Indeed, we could move straight to higher levels just through the power of our thought.

We also were connected to a number of "space-ships-commands" lead by the Orions with the support of our collaborators mainly from Sirius, Pleiades and Arthurian constellation. Each one of us, bringing different expertise and experience in particular fields of highly advanced technology.

Our initial tasks were to overtake certain Portals used by "The Darks", which control the planets vibrational functions. Once taken, some of them were de-activated by us, others adapted to serve our purposes. The challenge was to gain the control and to install our own technological structure. Once this was done, "The Darks" could not regain control as our technology was (and still is) far superior to theirs.

Our living in "Attalah-Thys" was busy but pleasant, peaceful and harmonious.

The base functioned as what is now known in "Earth-lands" as a "mega-city".

A striking bubble of crystal, under the darkness of a deep, silent and mysteriously "a-live" "One-Ocean".

So sparkly, full of light, amazingly bright.

A true statement of the legacy of our Origin; "Light & Love" contrasting with the surrounding "Darkness".

"All is One - All in One".

Peaceful place to be...

Once the first tasks were successfully completed, our missions became more diverse. We planted our crystal - bases in almost all Sacred Portals in "Earth-lands", some of them alongside today's most known and famous landmarks, temples and cities across the five continents.

A reminder: this is a story of love and compassion!

It is all about the heart and not the brain!

The message is to help you to switch on your "One-inner-Crystals" of "Uni-versal" love and light!

Enlightenment!

Once the initial phases were successfully implemented, some of us would have to live within the humans as to teach them the way to the stars.

It was a very dangerous mission for us. Those who volunteered to take part would have to downgrade, again!

The risks were very high. There was a serious consequence of which was to be caught in to the mankind vibrational system that would give "The Darks" the opportunity to take partial control over our freedom.

We had to follow some ground rules as to avoid this insertion to happen .Basically, those living amongst mankind had to follow all "Uni-versal" laws, respect the laws of mankind and ultimately never, ever have any physical relationship with the humans. To break one of the sacred rules, consciously or not, willingly or not, would take us to the "hamster-wheel".

Excited about such noble mission, Ahrgyan and I volunteered to be more directly involved with life in "Earth-lands".

We had each other, our ideals of love and "frahc-ether-nity", the support of the Orions and our friendly galactic allies.

With all of that in place, what could go wrong? We were so confident in succeeding!

I can tell you now that having that such naive assumption was our first big mistake!

To date, my romantic heart still wants to keep believing that love and compassion prevails above everything!

But I would learn at some point in future that love in "Earth-lands" is a complicated matter!

Back to then,

"The One and Uni-ted ", "Attalah -Thys" started experiencing division in its higher commands.

Some of us started to assume, like "The Darks", that the pace of human learning to become superior beings of light could be accelerated. As a consequence, they altered the nature of basic "Uni-versal" laws of evolution. Like "The Darks", they saw themselves as superior to any other kind. They wanted to impose their power to bring more light back to the "The-One". They were referred to as "The Rectus".

What "The Rectus" seemed to forget was that this was against the "The-One" principles based on" Uni-versal" causal laws.

The creation of the division of the "Uni-Thy" started to cause serious imbalances in "Earth-lands" vibrational dimensions at physical and "non-physical" levels.

In order to stop the imbalances caused by "The Rectus", a dissident group was formed.

They were called the "The Rebellys". Although their intentions were genuinely good, they also ended up breaking the "Uni-versal" rules in order to pursue what they believed it was right.

The remaining of us, who were not involved with either these two groups, conservatively abandoned the "Attalah-Thys' project". They returned to the Orion's commands around "Earth-lands" under the guidance of our associates Sirius, Pleiades and Arturos.

"Attalah-Thys" was "de-activated" by the "Elder Galactic Council" in the attempt to minimize the catastrophic events that would follow in Heaven and "Earth-Lands" as a consequence of the imbalances caused by our "own-One-people".

Another "Uni-versal" law: To every action taken, there is a "re-action" established!

Broken vows from us, "One-Star-Light" with the "The-One"!

Broken vows from us, "One-Star-Light "with our guardians, the Orions!

Broken vows from us, "One-Star-Light" with our galactic neighbours' friends!

Broken vows from us, "One-Star-Light" with us "One-Star-Light".

Broken vows from us with some of our "frahc-eter-nals" (meaning something like friends in the "One-Star-Light world"!).

And for myself....

The saddest moment of my entire existence...

Broken vows with my "One-Star-Light-prince" Ahrgyan...

How could this ever happened?

"One is One", that is our belief! Soul mates are forever "One"!

My then principles of rectitude and "The-One" justice led me to fight against "The Rectus", who betrayed our mission. It was clear in my mind that this was the right way to go. We had to regain the focus of our mission, we could not just let it go. I stood up with "The Rebellys".

On the other hand, Ahrgyan had the view that it was not up to us to take "The-One" justice into our own hands. For him and many others, we should respect the "Uni-versal "laws and not go against them nor harm our own kind or any other kind; nor harm any other living and non-living being.

He was devastated with my choice. He stayed a little behind from the returning group in an attempt to persuade me to go with him. For the first time since Creation, we were to go separate ways.

Free will as they call in "Earth-lands"!

"One is One-Self - One-Self is One".

Ahrgyan left to take another mission in "Earth-lands", but in other dimensions. He promised he would come back for me at a "later-time" once order was "re-established". Until then, we would lose contact.

To date, this "later-time" has not yet happened!

He joined one of the Orion-Sirius commands located in the superior orbs around to the lands of "Egyh - P- Thys" and surrounding areas.

In this mean time, I should be strong enough not to fall into the "hamster-wheel-trap"!

I could not believe that my "One-Star-Light-prince" was leaving me, giving up on our mission. Moreover, I could not even see this coming, as in my heart and soul, we were meant to be together forever and ever.

As our vibrational energy levels were so low in "Earth-lands", I experienced for the first time the pain of a broken heart. Ooops that hurts! BIG TIME!

Still, I could not leave all behind for him as he could not stay for me.

For both of us, our ideals of helping mankind to experience love and compassion were so important, that we have to put aside our most valuable treasure: Our eternal love!

Broken vows!!!

However, we both knew that "Uni-versal" laws prevail: "One is One".

No matter of time, no matter of destiny, and no matter of mission: "One is Half - Half is One".

I felt like a shooting star... Going down very fast.... So alone!

So be it!

"One is Light - Dark is One"

ONE
GOES AROUND
ONE
:
ONE
COMES AROUND
ONE

CHAPTER EIGHT OF TWELVE

The "hamster-wheel"

"One goes around One - One comes around One"

Alone and hurt, I focused on my mission. We, "The Rebellys" were many and "uni-ted" by our "Earth-lands-cause". Some of us were disguised, pretending to be with "The Rectus"; others taking on more specific missions against them.

We, "The Rebellys" just wanted to "re-install" order! At the time, this was my belief when I sided with them. However, we did not anticipated that, engaging in such fight, we were helping to build chaos in "Earth-lands" with catastrophic consequences.

Loyal to my group, I used my background to support some projects on bio- energy and bio-genetics so we could develop more resources. I disclosed some core ancient knowledge to some of our scientists as to sustain the guidelines of the original mission we were initially trusted to implement in "Earth-lands" by the Orions.

It was my second big mistake since living in "Earth-Lands". My "own-One-colleagues" betrayed me by using the new information to testing in living creatures. I found out this terrible news in a shocking way!

I am not even going into those memories as they were too horrific to describe.

I just could not believe, what they were doing was so cruel, emotionless! They became like "The Rectus", like "The Darks": selfish, centred and disheartened!

I was then experiencing new and frightening feelings like guilt, despair, loneliness, hurt. I did not know where to go, what to do, who to trust.

My human eyes cried non-stop. How did I let that happen???

Everything I believed with my soul was somehow quite not true in the hostile "Earth-lands" world.

Love, loyalty, compassion, integrity, rectitude, "frahc-eter-nity" ... Light!

My inner world became so afraid of being attacked and hurt!

Afraid of my "One-self" and that the powers I had could potentially cause harm to others, I created a "glass-dome" in which I am living for thousands of "Earth-land-years".

It is like an energy field in which I am an island in my "One-inner-self". All my memory, my background, my knowledge, my "One-being -essence" are dormant so they could not harm a living-being ever again!

This is all too much to express in human language....

Deep sadness, despair...

Lost and feeling like I have "no-where" to go, "no-One" to trust, I decided to experiment with the excitement and distractions of human living. I broke the number one rule and all the other rules at the same time.

So there I was, trapped in the "hamster-wheel"! I failed the Orions; I did not stand by my "One-Star-Light-prince" and finally, unwillingly, I brought suffering to humankind!

This was the punishment I thought I deserved! As you can see that in itself was my link to the "hamster- wheel", as I felt I no longer deserved my "One-Star-Light" status!

With the pleasures of human life, there I was in the "hamster-wheel".

So far, I had hundreds of life cycles in it. Different continents, countries, languages, relationships, husbands, loves, lovers, professions, causes, families, dimensions. So you name it!

Since then, all of my lives were linked and sustained by my feelings of guilt and hurt.

In all of them, I was desperately trying to make "Justice" with my own hands with the view helping humankind to evolve. At personal level, in all of my lives, I tried to find a prince that would love me enough to rescue me out of the "hamster- wheel" and take me back home!

Eight thousand years, and still counting.... To find out that my causes were all flawless, my princes were all frogs!!!

True love cannot be, whilst we are in the trap!

In the "hamster-wheel-land", love is based on the illusion of material living, to include emotional feelings that we perceive as love but it is too dense to be it!

There are so many distractions in "Earth-lands".

The price of "Earth-lands-illusion-assets" like concepts of love, lust, justice, prosperity and happiness is too high to pay in the "Uni-verse-banks"!

My debts became higher and higher! The "pay-back" credits are also at a high cost and even more difficult to get! We have to work really hard to earn them!

Trying to succeed in "Earth-lands", I created love, lovers, and princes. Some of them were real princes with no heart; others I crowned myself; some I pretended were princes. All created illusions of what I could still sense about true love.

The "Reality" was and still is that a "One-Star-Light-princess" cannot consort in the "hamster-wheel"!

Trying to succeed, I took part in many wars, causes, justice! Some of them were way too big, others pointless; others powerless.

The "Reality" is that a "One-Star-Light princess" cannot reign in the "hamster- wheel"!

I know this now... I knew this then...

However, "Knowledge" in itself was not enough to understand....

Hence, I kept trying, running in circles in the "hamster-wheel".... Again and again....

Sometimes, I run so fast to the point of exhaustion.

I kept trying to find a place in which things can happen the way my "One-Star-Light- heart" intended!

A place in which justice could exist; a place in which human kind would live free and happy!

It was all an illusion...

I went "no-where", I got "no-where"! I am "no-where"!

I can tell I feel the void ... My light is weak, I feel so lonely.

I miss my people; I miss the Orions; I miss my "One-Star-Light-prince"... BIG TIME

I look at the stars, they seem so far away.

There was "One-time", I was "One" of them...

And life continues.... The "Uni-verse" still rules, it is all here and there...

All "the same" but "the same" for me now is all different!

"One goes around One - One comes around One"

ONE
IS ONE-SELF
:
ONE-SELF IS ONE

CHAPTER NINE OF TWELVE

Realms of time: The awakening

"One is One-Self" - "One-Self is One"

Some of you may find the next lines difficult to understand.

Another reminder that we are not talking about conventional logic!

It is all about love! It is about our complicated human hearts. It is "never-ever" straight forward! All I know is that in "Earth - lands" sometimes love means hurt and sorrow!

Enlightenment !

We need light to see through darkness; we need freedom of our soul to overcome "Earth-lands- love-traps"! As much as they can bring us the pleasure, they have the power to add endless runs in the "hamster -wheel".

It is very tiring...

It is very hurtful...

This path cost me a great number of loose rounds in the "hamster-wheel"!

"One" has many layers of light. "One" has many lives at the same time.

Remember: "One is One"!

Back to the story....

Like the vows of first communion with " The-One" once you grounded in "Earth-lands-living", I had to go throughout the conflict of leaving behind the ever running circles of the "hamster-wheel" or facing the unknown of finding my way back to the Stars; both options very frightening!

But I was, I am and I always will be a "One-Star-Light-princess-fighter"!

Fear cannot be!

I finally understood I no longer belonged to the "hamster-wheel".

It was time to ask for the help of the Masters Orions!

I wanted to come back to the way to the Stars!

I wanted my "One-self" back!

I wanted my mission in "Earth-lands" back!

Finally, I wanted my only and "One-Star-Light-prince" back.

When "One" ask "The-One", from the core of "One's soul" for help, "The-One" responds immediately with exactly what is needed!

"The-One" is always there for his children.

I looked at the stars and cried for help....

And help came to my pathway in all sorts and kinds!

From "up and above" golden lights travelled from "The-One" source to my "One-self", me!

From an alternative space-time, Yhkhree -Ra, a future version of my "One-self" came to the rescue.

The concept of "One" helping "One-self" is still to be assimilated in "Earth-lands".

Simply describing it, the "synchroniser effect" occurs when "One" can be with their "One-self", in parallel and yet concurrent "space-time".

Extra- protection was needed until all of my "One-self" became a sacred "Uni-Thy".

I cannot wait to be able to fly again, free and above the skylines...

Flying ... Ah ... This is one of the most wonderful feelings of freedom that "One" can experience in both, "Earth-lands" or sidereal spaces.

The Orions also stepped up to help me!

So came to the rescue a very close "One-Star-Light", my "best -" frahc-eter-nal".Her name is Yhnnah - Kah. She came from far away Stars.

So a number of special" frahc-eter-nals", who from different realms, contributed for the success of securing my freedom.

For all the group, this was a sacred opportunity of rescuing "One" back to "Light-ways"!

It was a complex and delicate mission.

Redemption, this is the only way out of the "hamster-wheel". "One" has to be of strong will power and determination.

I was in this running for eight thousands of "Earth-lands" years.

Those were no longer.

Love, forgiveness, detachment of the Ego, compassion.

Combined, those elements can make miracles in Heaven and "Earth-lands".

It is easy to fall into the "hamster-wheel trap"; extremely difficult to get out!

There were consequences though.... and eternal scars as a reminder of times in which I was lost in my own illusions.

Takes time to overcome this process ... And it is not entirely free of "Earth-lands-commitments" previously made with family and friends, opponents and so on...

During one of the most difficult times in this process, the Orions gave me a prayer to help me to go through the toughest moments in which I needed everything I had in my "One-self" to fight against the temptations and the illusions of "Earth-lands-life".

With the Orions' permission, I now share with you the sacred wording of the higher realms.

For the "Ones" who are able to embrace its meanings, in the name of the Light, this is indeed a gift from Heaven!

For the "others-Ones" who yet are not ready to embrace Light, it is also a gift from Heaven!

Keep it for later as a gift to be unveiled in a different "space-time", a time in which you will be ready to appreciate it!

One day- One time....

A Prayer for Protection:

From my being, in the expansion of the "Uni-verse", I give to all and everything, the Light and "Uni-versal" Love.

Everything that belongs to me, belongs to the "Uni-verse".

I don't give authorisation to any being to extract from my soul what is mine; sustained and validated by the "Uni-versal" laws and rights.

The protection is within me.

"A-men".

"One is One-Self" - "One-Self is One"

ONE
IS COMPASSION
:
COMPASSION
IS ONE

CHAPTER TEN OF TWELVE

The Gardens of Redemption

"One is Compassion - Compassion is One"

Those were difficult times.

I was experiencing my symbolic "re-birth" as a "One-Star-Light", this time in "Earth-lands", which make the process very complicated.

It was very confusing as I was still living in a dense matter, surrounded by illusion and connected to people who were still running in the "hamster-wheel".

And indeed, the contradiction of being taken out of the "hamster-wheel" but at the same time having to keep living by it.

Quite a challenge, I must say!

I was so used to running in circles in the "hamster-wheel". That was my way of living!

Looking at it from the outside now, it seems very surreal to me!

It was very outlandish to then observe the "hamster-wheel" as "un-real" as it was my reality for thousands of "Earth-lands-years"!

Memories, emotions, "relation-ships" that organically would "be-come" something else like "new-One-missions" of "under-standing", acceptance and compassion!

Hard work indeed for a "One-Star-Light" who has been under "mankind -living" for so long...

It was reassuring though, to remember that once you are "One" you will always be "One"!

Redemption is the word that the cosmic masters kept saying to me!

Redemption of your heart! Redemption of your soul!

Believe in yourself! Believe in miracles!

My thoughts of a "One-Star-Light-rebel-princess" were:

Very well, the point of believing is easy to assimilate! Quite inspiring to the soul!

The fundamental question is: How can "One" see those wishes happening in "living-times"?

I could not find the answer nor, as we say in "Earth-lands": to see the light through the end of the tunnel...

I knew one thing: I needed help. I needed those miracles to happen!

And fast....

I did not want to lose this once more opportunity given to me!

This is not the time for panic or failure!

I will find a way of overcoming this moment in time...

I will succeed!

To this present time, I still have contact with some of the "Rebellys" from "Attalah-Thys". We continued to be "frach-ether-nals". Like me, many of "One" ended up in the "hamster-wheel". We are "One" for "One-other". This is one of the ways that the "Uni-verse" supports us in the lower realms. By helping "each-One-other" we can build up the strength to keep us well-balanced and strong whilst in the crazy running of the "hamster-wheel".

We kept meeting "One-another", every now and then in different life-times. Our "One-Star-Light-souls" can sense "One's "presence even when it is not known at our "human- conscious -level ". We know that we can trust and help "each-One-other" as we go along through cyclic journeys in "Earth-lands-life".

Luckily at this "time-life," I had the support of "One "of my closest "frahc-eter-nal". His name is Mahrak - Tuhs- Ahnak.

Since our time in "Attalah-Thys", we both had many "Earth-lands-missions" together. The most prominent in my memory was the one in which Mahrak was a "Temple - Master" in the lands of "Egyh -P-Thys" and I was his apprentice.

You may think: How come a "One-Star-Light-princess" can be "One" of "apprentice-ship?

Here is the answer for you:

As a One-Star-Light-princess", I would hold special knowledge and powers like very few across the "Uni-verse". However, as a rough diamond stone, I had to be dilapidated to become a beautiful, shiny, unique and precious stone.

So, the "Uni-verse-Masters", at higher and lower realms, have in me , the rumble "One-Star-Light-rebel-princess" , who lives in "Earth-lands", a challenging mission to be completed!

I can tell you that knowing my "One-self", I wish them good luck! It is hard work indeed!

If they have one attribute that can help them to succeed in supporting my evolution is "PATIENCE".

Whilst in " Egyh - P- Thys-lands, Mahrak and I were both locked in the "hamster -wheel". However, at that point we were still connected to the Orions by taking on missions in the dense matter that they themselves could not do it.

At that time, some of the humans would perceive our presence as ambassadors of their Gods in "Earth -lands" with special " body- mind-souls-healing-powers".

In reality, we were only part of a group of "One-Star-Light" trying to redeem ourselves by giving something good and worthy back to humanity.

Back to the future, in the redemption's time, here and now, I was in trouble again, filling the void of being in the limbo between the "hamster- wheel" and the way to the stars.

Awkward place to be, indeed!

Mahrak came to my "One-rescue"! He led me to find the Gardens of Redemption.

This is a place in "space-time", in which I could go and start a catharsis process in the twelve energy fields of my "Earth-lands-body".

Progressively and in time, this process will take me more and more out of the protective glass dome I created in the past. Once purified and counter-balanced, I finally will be re-integrated to my "One-Star-Light-self".

During these little but "ether-nal" moments in the gardens of redemption, I was able to refill my energies, meet briefly with my friends of Orion and most important to connect with my "One-Star-Light-prince!" That was so special! Again, no "Earth-lands-words" to describe this feeling!

If you are "One" like me, once you connect to my words, you will be able to feel and understand how immense is this feeling of Love inside me!

If you are "One" like me, once you connect to my feelings, you will be able to feel and understand that you have the same feeling inside you as well.

Yes, Love is in you! How is for you to realise that?

In the moment you come to this realisation, you will understand what is Love in its essence. That's exactly when you consciously will connect to your journey to the stars!

Do not worry! You will not be in this journey on your own!

Your "frach-ether-nals" will come from far distances to be your "One-guardians".

You will have then to find your own "Gardens of Redemption" in which concepts such as "com-passion", "for-give-ness", "under-standing", "un-conditional love", acceptance will become more than words for you but your way of being ... and living!

May the Angels of Light bless this moment in time of yours!

"A-men".

"One is Compassion - Compassion is One"

ONE
LOOKS FOR ONE
:
ONE FINDS ONE

CHAPTER ELEVEN OF TWELVE

Time is no longer

"One looks for One - One finds One"

There are many ways of "One" inter- connecting to "One-Other".

Even in "Earth-lands"...

As I , increasingly begin to recall the sacred teachings , I begin to be conscious of the more "One" empowers" One-self" to embrace Light more "One" will be able to realise the profusion of resources we carry on within our soul.

This powerful energy is itself hugely spirited, bright and uplifting.

I, Thyan-B, am now on the way to re-connect to the "One" inside my "One-self".

This quest seems to me as super-colossal as my journey from "The One" to "Earth-lands".

I am fighting to shift from a shooting-star to a raising-star.

All back to the beginning... This time though, I am not running in circles but spiralling up to Light.

That's the key that opens up the doors to what I really am: My "One -Self".

I can tell you that this place is beautiful, serene, and harmonious. Many of us feel scared to face it.

Certainly, I am!

It is almost like we are denying to our "One-selves" the right to be happy, contained and free!

It is time know for mankind to understand and embrace its inner powers of Light.

The only way to find our "One-selves" is "not beyond " ; it is not outside; it is not in reach of any point of reference. The only way to find our "One-selves" is within!

Understand this and each "One" of you", each "One" of us, will be taking the first steps to "dis-continue" the triggers implemented by "The Darks" to "de-celerate" our "One" natural progression as a "Being of Light".

Based on the "Uni-versal" law of Creation, with property, I can say that, evolving to "be-come" "One" of Light is a matter of fact! It will happen!

One day ... One time…

It is just up to each "individual-One" to choose when will be the time to experience peace and joy outside the "hamster- wheel"!

Once you be able of finding your "One-self" you will be then able to find many of your "One-other-selves". You will be then living in a world of "frach-ether-nity", harmony and expansion.

My "One-Star-Light-soul" comes to its beginning...

My "human-soul" is" be-coming" a bright star!

It is all now mixed and an integrated part of my "One".

From Creation to the here and now, I now comprehend that I am no longer a germinal "One-Star-Light-princess." I grew seeds of Love and Light from different kinds that are now well-matured throughout different "space-times".

I Thyan-B, have now in my genetic print the legacy of so many constellations, stars and planets to include my beloved "Earth-lands".

By descending, I "be-came" partly human.

By ascending, you are" be-coming" a star!

In the diversity of the divine Cosmos we all "be-long"; in the essence of things we are all equal; we are all "Ones" of pure Light.

We are all "One" and part of the "The-One".

I Thyan-B, have now a story to tell you...

It is time to continue my mission in "Earth-lands", which was long commissioned, which is of spreading the seeds of Light.

"One looks for One - One finds One"

ONE
AND ONE
:
ONE AND
ONE

CHAPTER TWELVE OF TWELVE

The end of the endings...

"One and One - One and One"

As we land in the last chapter of the tales of "One-Star-Light", I guess we all (including my "One-self") are wondering about how this tale of a "One-Star-Light" is going to end?

Most of us (including my "One-self") are expecting a happy ending; the "fairy-tale-ending" in which, after all the drama, the prince and his princess finally find "each-One-other"; They kiss and stay happy "to-get-her", "for-ever" and ever again!

However, like for each " One "of you, my journey through the chapters was a world of experiences, feelings, emotions and wishes that led me to reflect and learn even more than words can describe.

That is what our sacred Life is all about: learning from every single moment in time, making the most of it, sharing and disseminating "our-One- experiences", growing together and supporting "each-One-other".

Compassion ...Redemption ... Forgiveness...

That is what our sacred Mission is all about: giving the best we have inside us, being "com-passionate", respecting the "Uni-verse" laws, respecting "each-Other", being part of a world of continuum Love and Light.

Ultimately, our sacred Truth, is to free the "One" inside ourselves....

That is the only way to finding "ether-nal" happiness.

That is the only way that will take us to our "happy-ending" and at the same time the way to our new beginnings in the realms of the "The-One".

Tears come to my eyes in the "here and now" whilst I am trying to translate all my feelings into "Earth-lands-words". As the words flow into my soul and transform into living actions, I feel overwhelmed by a sublime deep sense of honour and gratitude.

Honour and Gratitude for all and everything that the "Uni-verse" has granted to me as a "One-Star-Light -princess", as an Orion, as an "Earth-lands-citizen".

Honour and Gratitude for those who believed in me; gratitude for those who cherished me; gratitude for those who were my "frach-ether-nals".

Honour and Gratitude for those who betrayed me; gratitude for those who hurt me; gratitude for those who were my opponents.

Remember:"One is compassion- Compassion is One".

I wish you can be " re-united "to the essence of these "action-words "too so your heart and soul can be opened to the unknown; to "life-doors" that will lead all and each "One" of you to a blessed evolution!

I hope that my "One" story open your "One-ways" to connect to your "One-story" so the "Uni-verse" can expand in its integrity. Enlightenment!

That is my "One-Mission".

As for me and my "One-Star-Light-prince", I realised that the happy ending I was pursuing belongs to the illusions of the "hamster-wheel's world"!

I am no longer there, therefore I can truly understand now that there was never an ending...

We just had a physical break ... But our hearts were together all the time!

A true love is "never-ending" therefore it will never have an ending in itself.

That's how it is ... "For-ever".

I know from my heart, that one day, we are both "come -ing "home.

We are going "to-get-there " together as we always have been.

When I look to the "night-sky", all the ways point to our star!

It is so beautiful! So bright ... Magnificent ... What a place to be!

We love "each-other" always throughout "all-ways"....

Probably you are thinking: So, is this the ending?

My final answer to you is:

There are many "One-ways" but there is only "One" ending....

The "One" ending is the same for all of us: "The-One"

Follow the Light and find your star!

May the Angels of Light

Guide you; protect you...

Guide you, protect you....

Guide you, protect you....

"A-men".

"One and One - One and One"

E-L-P - Y-R & T-B-A-N- Earth-lands - Fall - MMXIII -AD

ONE
IS ALL
:
ALL IS
ONE